SNOW STRINGS ATTACHED

To Yasmin
Live your Goldilocks
fantasy
Melody Mode

MELODY MODE

Copyright © 2024 by Melody Mode

All rights reserved. No part of this book may be reproduced in any form or by any electronic or mechanical means, including information storage and retrieval systems, without written permission from the author, except for the use of brief quotations in a book review. This is a work of fiction. Names, characters, places and incidents are either the product of the author's imagination or used factiously. Any resemblance to actual persons, living or dead, events or locales, is entirely coincidental.

Editing & Formatting: Cassie at Weaver Way Author Services

Cover: Soren Covers

ISBN: 9798322697053 (Paperback)

BOOKS BY MELODY

A Touch of Heaven

Snow Strings Attached

COMING SOON

A Touch of Sin (Book 2 of the Unholy Bastards – Coming Summer 2024

Captured by Desire – Coming Autumn 2024

The Twisted Brothers – Coming Winter 2024

To the ladies that wished they fell asleep in the wrong cabin just like goldilocks, with one minor change. Those three bears were men who knew nothing about purity and innocence and instead only knew sin, debauchery and danger.

AUTHOR NOTE

This novella was previously published with the charity Snowed In Anthology. It is now newly published as a standalone novella with two new unseen chapters.

CONTENT WARNINGS

This is a reverse heram novella that features one girl and three guys.

This book treads the line of dark desires, including knife play, breath play, blood play, spit play, being tied up and ruthlessly fucked. There is also discussion of murder of a family member by one of the main men in this tale.

Do not read this story if you have any light in you. This is for those who seek true debauchery.

PROLOGUE

*A*re you like me and crave adventure?
Something risky and life-changing?

Well let me tell you, I never could have imagined how much that winter would have changed my life. I wanted to be a musician, you know, and my dream came true after one weekend of getting *all* the inspiration I needed.

My debut album went pretty high on the charts, and of course, BookTok was a key factor in that. I didn't even know what that was at one point, but let me tell you…they were more than happy to hear my songs that delved into the dark, dirty, and depraved. Hell, I was more than happy to tell them, but no one knew what inspired my music career.

I'm about to sit down with Millie Jones, interviewer to the stars. I always insist on having any questions sent over to me beforehand, and one of them is what inspired my music. Of course, everyone asks that, and usually, I give them a sly wink and keep my story to myself. After all, the boys that, quite frankly, gave me the weekend of my life deserved some privacy.

However, the flowers sitting on my dressing room table that

were delivered to the studio today tell me they know my songs are about them. Over twelve dozen black and hot pink roses dawn the room, black for them and pink for me. I have fuchsia streaks running through my hair now. After that weekend, I changed. They corrupted my very being and I needed a change from the long blonde hair I had that encounter.

Devin, Zane, and Levi—my dark demons that corrupted my very soul in a weekend of fire, debauchery, and depravity. All four of us agreed it was one weekend and one weekend only but as my fingers graze the card wishing me luck, I know it will be a weekend that no one guy will ever match.

"Five minutes, Nova." My assistant calls out, her head poking around the door as she smiles at me. I nod, smiling. Maybe this will be the night I tell all, let my secrets loose.

I walk out the door and down to the studio, taking a seat in one of the chairs in front of the camera. The production company is doing a live piece on this year's hottest stars, and I'm one of them. I shake my head; it's still surreal to me that little ol' me is going to be named as that.

Millie walks over to me, takes a seat in front of me and gives me one of those typical LA smiles. You know the kind I mean, all fake teeth and Botox, I moved here about six months ago when my music career began to take off, but LA looks shiny from a distance. When you're in the muck, you realize that shine is fake. Fake tan, fake nails, fake boobs even. I sometimes miss my hometown, but I couldn't ever move back. Millie leans forward, extending her hand and shaking mine, breaking me away from my thoughts. Someone starts counting down, and then it's show time.

"I'm here with Nova—one of this year's hottest new stars who not only took over social media with her music but made a lot of women very ecstatic." She says to the camera before smiling over at me, her perfect teeth showing. "Huge fan, Nova, your song One Long Tease—well, let's just say I was more than happy with my husband after he listened to that song." She gives me a wink and a light laugh. She's not the first person to say that to me.

"You should make sure he listens to my next one," I reply with ease. It's so funny to me that I used to be so nervous about anyone listening to my music. This one would have made me blush and sink in my seat, but confidence and sexuality ooze from me now. Those boys made me who I am today.

"I'll make sure he does! So, Nova, your lyrics are obviously very…provocative." She giggles lightly, and I smile back innocently. "I think we're all hoping there is some filthy, sordid story behind them. I mean, the thing everyone wants to know is this—where does your inspiration come from? The song One Weekend with The Devils—did that really happen?"

I run my tongue over my lips, slowly biting my lower one before leaning forward. "You want to know a secret?" I ask her before winking at the camera. "Okay, here it is…"

CHAPTER ONE

12 MONTHS AGO

I sit on the stool, a glass of wine on the side as I look at my keyboard aimlessly, willing the music to come but nothing does. I sigh, picking up my glass and looking out the window. The snow is really coming down now.

I rented a cabin in the mountains for the weekend just before Christmas. No distractions, just me and my music. But since my breakup with Danny, I just haven't found my muse. Hell, it seems like it runs away from me, screaming because I've been feeling sorry for myself. I don't want to be an artist who writes about heartbreak, but that's all that's been on my mind recently. I studied music for years, but finding your voice is something no one can teach you. It's hard to find your voice, though, when you're from a humdrum town where you're known as the good country girl. I crave excitement and adventure— I know I'm a cliché. Yet here I sit, looking at the snow, feeling like I need something more.

The snowstorm is getting thicker, and it's basically a blizzard outside. The cabin is warm, though. The roaring fire next to the Christmas tree that's artfully decorated in tinsel heats the blood pumping through my veins. I step away from the window and instead take a seat on the couch, deciding to take a break from writing for a bit. My eyes are heavy, the drive was really long, and the wine definitely makes me sleepy. Danny always used to say I could never hold my drink. I either went crazy hyper with spirits or drowsy with wine, *asshole,* and that's the last thought I have before I feel my eyes closing and sleep taking me over.

I wake with a start, feeling like someone is watching me. Glancing around, I discover I am right. There are three pairs of gorgeous eyes staring down at me, attached to what can only be described as the finest specimens of men god put on this earth. I should scream; the smirks on their faces should make me uncomfortable. Yet I'm sitting here silently with my mouth open like some idiot. Shit, where is my fight-or-flight response? Why isn't it kicking in?

"Well, well, boys, looks like Goldilocks has been sleeping in our cabin." Honey-brown eyes bare into my soul as he speaks teasingly. Blue Eyes speaks up next.

"I'd rather have her sleeping in my bed." He chuckles. My eyes flick to the guy who hasn't spoken yet, but he doesn't say anything. Instead, he just tilts his head at me, grinning.

"Is there a reason you're in our cabin, Goldilocks?" the first guy asks.

I sit up with a bolt, spilling my wine on my jeans. "Fuck! Uh, what do you mean your cabin? I booked this for the weekend. I think you have the wrong house. You…you need to leave now." I try to sound strong and convincing, yet the tremor in my voice lets me down.

Blue Eyes laughs. "No, Goldy, this cabin belongs to us. You have the wrong one, but there's no need for you to leave just yet." He takes a seat opposite me, lounging in the armchair, and my mind runs round in circles.

"I'm Devin, this is Zane." Honey Eyes looks toward Blue Eyes in the chair.

"I'm Levi," the silent one finally speaks. For the first time, I look over each one to figure out how much trouble I am in.

Okay, Honey Eyes is Devin, who is dressed in jeans and a black leather jacket, but damn, this guy is huge. I'm talking muscles and bulging biceps. He laughs as I look him over, knowing I'm taking him in. I just hope I'm not drooling.

My eyes flick over to Zane lounging in the chair. He's like a big cat—tall, lean, and he's looking at me like I'm prey about to be devoured. His bright ocean-blue eyes catch me in a trap, and I have a feeling that happens to a lot of girls. I can see tattoos creeping up his neck, out of his T-shirt, and down his arm. His chestnut hair is styled to perfection.

Last but not least, Levi. Dark brown eyes—almost black—and they make my breath catch. This guy, out of all of them, is the most dangerous, I can tell. There's something about him. His tongue runs over his lips, and I catch a tongue piercing, making me swallow hard. If this wasn't potentially a dangerous scenario, I would think this is a porno with how fucking hot they all are.

"I uh…I'm Nova."

"Pretty name," Devin drops casually before walking into the kitchen.

"I'm sorry, I don't know what happened. I must have got the wrong address; and the door was unlocked, and the fire was already burning. I just figured the landlord had set this place up for me."

Zane laughs deeply. "Goldilocks definitely suits you. You walk into a house and make yourself right at home. We went into town to get supplies, but yes, you have the wrong address. This is our cabin and always has been."

"I'm sorry. I'll pack my stuff and leave now." I jump up with a start, and Levi grabs my wrist and pulls me against him. *Scream Nova*, I think to myself, yet all I can do is wonder how those gray-black eyes would look on top of me.

"Not happening. You can't drive in this storm, and we won't be held responsible for letting you get yourself killed out here."

"I can't just stay…"

"Actually, you're going to have to. The roads blocked. The snow caused a slide, and a couple of trees blocked the road. We had to leave our car and walk through, and it's got a hell of a lot worse now."

Devin walks back in with four beers, holding one out to me, and it's only then that Levi lets go of my wrist. He plays with his piercing between his teeth as he backs away and sits on the coffee table.

Do I trust these guys…

"How do I know you've not put a roofie in here?" I nod toward the beer being held out to me. Devin chuckles, handing the rest of the beers out before taking a gulp of mine. He wraps his arm around my waist, pulling me close suddenly with a jolt.

"Trust me, Nova, we don't like our girls unconscious; we like to make them scream our names when we're inside of her. And yes, Goldilocks, in case you're wondering, we do mean at the same time." He gives me a wink before letting go and taking a seat on the couch. He throws his jacket on the side as he stretches out, I watch a vein pop out as his muscles bulge and flex in front of me. "You going to sit or stand there all night?"

I swallow, taking a seat next to him, realizing his arm is behind me. "Aren't you guys brothers or something?"

Zane nearly spits out his beer. "Do we look like brothers?"

"Well…no…"

"We're friends, Nova, but we do consider ourselves brothers, just not in that sense." Levi grins, and he exchanges a look with Zane. I have a feeling there's a secret there that I'll never know.

"That's your immediate thought, though? Not the fact we like to fuck a girl at the same time?" Devin tips his head to the side like he's assessing if I'm going to bolt at that.

"Hey, whatever turns you on. I don't judge." I shrug, taking a swig of my beer. "It's not like we don't all have our kinks."

"And you, Blondie… What kinks do you have?" I smirk back, strangely feeling comfortable with these guys. No doubt they're trouble, but somehow, I don't think they are to me.

"Hey, that's for me to know and you to dot dot dot." I laugh.

Devin leans in, running his fingers through a strand of my hair. "Is that an invitation?" he whispers, and I watch the other two exchange another look. "Because you really shouldn't say things like that to strangers, especially us."

CHAPTER TWO

*M*y body shivers, *fuck why does that turn me on so much?* I'm kinky, sure, but three random hot strangers...that's never crossed my mind. Devin grabs the beer from my hand, placing it on the table before his hand goes to my neck. The coldness of the bottle is still there, making me shiver as he pulls me closer. He smirks as his lips land inches away from mine.

"Tell me something, Nova, has a guy ever really truly satisfied you? Explored every single kink you know you have? Helped you discover new ones that make your body sing for him?" I feel the sofa dip behind me, hot breath on my neck appearing. I feel Zane's hand on my arm, stroking it.

A small whimper leaves me as my mind empties. I can't even remember the question. The boys' senses invade mine, and my body trembles at what could happen here tonight. God, would I really let this happen? *Stupid question, Nova,* I think. Three hot guys wanting to fuck me, of course I would!

Zane's fingers continue to trail up and down my arm. "He asked you a question," he whispers, his voice low and gravelly

"I can't remember the question," I say honestly, and Devin chuckles. He lets go of my neck, leaning back on the sofa. Zane pulls me onto his lap; his fingers go to my chin as he tilts my head to him.

"Silly girl." He pulls my chin toward him before he claims my lips in a fiery kiss that makes me melt into him. I kiss back just as passionately, our tongues playing in ecstasy as he wraps his hand in my hair, pulling on it hard and making me yelp as he rips my lips from his. He grins as I pout, "I can't be greedy, Nova, no matter how much I want to… Why don't you go and give Levi a taste of you." I look at Levi, and he winks at me from where he's perched on the coffee table in front of us. I nod, and Zane lets go of my hair.

I get up, slowly walk over to Levi, and stand in front of him. He grabs my hips, turning me around to face the others before pulling me into his lap. My back is against his solid chest as I look at the other two. His hands work over my thighs, pulling them apart as I moan in anticipation of where his hands might wander. His fingers toy with my leggings as they roam up and down my thigh.

"Tell me, Goldilocks…how wet is this pussy right now?" His fingers go up to the waistband of my pants, giving them a tug before ripping them apart in one go until my baby pink thong is exposed. His fingers immediately pull it to one side as he teases me. Running his fingers up and down my soaked lips before teasing my hole.

I tilt my head to look at him, breathing heavily and shakily before he slips two fingers inside of me, making me gasp in pleasure. Wet sounds fill the room as he slowly teases me, stroking my pussy walls as he continues sliding his fingers in and out of me. My mind empties of all the dangerous thoughts. All I can focus on is how he feels inside of me, craving more.

"That's it, Nova, take my fingers like a good little slut. We need to get you ready for us." I moan in response. I've never been called a slut before, but it definitely turns me on in a way I couldn't dream of. I bite my lip, my eyes rolling back as his fingers explore my pussy.

"Open your eyes." He growls, and I do. "Look at you doing as you're told already." He pulls his fingers away from me, and before I can pout at the lost sensation, his fingers are in my mouth. "Suck." He orders, and I do, eagerly, in fact. Tasting myself on them before he pushes them further into my mouth, making me gag a little. My eyes begin to tear up, and he smirks at me. "That's it, you can do it." He pushes them even further as I feel his digits slip into my throat. A drop of saliva falls from my lips before he pulls his fingers away aggressively and kisses me with such intensity I can barely breathe.

I feel his fingers on the hem of my sweater as he breaks the kiss to pull it over my head and he tosses it to the side, resuming the kiss as quick as he can. He stands up, pulling me up with him as he rips my leggings again. Breaking the kiss once more to pull them off completely. "She tastes sweet." He grins. Looking at me as he wipes the smudged mascara from under my eyes.

Now that I am in just my thong and bra, I tremble, not from the cold but from the thought of these guys taking what they obviously desire from me.

"Come here, Nova," Devin orders.

I'm being passed between them, and honestly, I really don't mind. If anything, I want it more than anything I have ever wanted in my life. Devin pats his lap, and I straddle him. My thighs fall on either side of him as my hands curl against his chest. He kisses my forehead, and I frown. He laughs deeply. "Don't worry, gorgeous, I'll have my turn." He leans back against the couch. "Right now, I just want to look at you." His fingers run up the sides of my hips and stomach lightly, but he's not touching me where I want him to. I hear a note on my keyboard, and it's Levi.

"You play?" he asks, and I nod softly.

"I, uh, write my own music, but I'm a little blocked right now."

"Me too," he says softly as he nods his head.

He strolls back over to me, leaning down and kissing me, his tongue tasting sweet as he groans into my mouth. He pulls himself away and looks at Devin.

What the hell is happening right now?

"Dinner?" Devin asks, and Zane laughs.

"Sure. I'll start it now."

Devins hands grasp my ass, squeezing it before patting it. "Trust me, Goldilocks, you'll need your strength."

"But…"

His fingers land on my lips. "No buts, Nova. You need to eat first, then maybe if you beg like a good girl for us. We will play with you."

"I don't beg," I grit out between my teeth, slightly annoyed with this situation.

"Oh, trust me, you'll beg." He thrusts up his hips as he pulls me down on him. I feel how rock-hard he is, and by the way he feels, he's big. "You'll beg us to play with you, for all three of our cocks to be buried inside of you, and when you can't bare it any longer because you're so sensitive and you don't think you can come anymore, you'll beg us to stop. But Nova…we'll only stop when we want to."

CHAPTER THREE

Well, this is strangely awkward. Here I am, sitting in just my lingerie in a cabin in the mountains around a table with three guys who clearly want me, yet here we all are, politely eating. The boys have been talking about this club they own but I get the feeling it's not an actual club but more an underground type thing. It's clear these guys are bad news, yet here I am, wanting them so desperately to touch me I can barely swallow my food.

"Chase is booked against James again. He wanted a rematch," Levi says coolly.

The boys laugh. "Chase is a beast, man. He barely got up last time. Asher and Jax had to get in the ring to rip him off James."

Levi shrugs. "It's his funeral. He wants a rematch, and Chase agreed."

"Who's Chase?" I ask meekly.

Devin pats his lap, and I push my chair back to join him as he asked…well told. He holds a fry up to my lip, and I take it gladly. What is it about a guy feeding you that makes you feel safe? I think I just set females back about twenty years with that thought.

"Chase is an acquaintance back home. We went to high school together."

I nod. That couldn't have been more than a couple of years ago. These guys can't be much older than me, and I'm only twenty-one. Devin kisses my neck slowly, satisfied when I swallow.

"You guys own a boxing ring?" I ask, and Levi laughs.

"Not exactly, but you don't need to know the details, sweetheart. The less you know about us, the better." He pushes my plate toward me, and I roll my eyes, picking up another fry and eating it.

"Good girl," Levi says, and I find myself blushing.

Zane looks over to me and chuckles, taking a bite of his burger. "If that makes you blush, you better prepare yourself for what we have in store for you." Devin pats my thong between my thighs, and I whimper as he pats just over my clit. "So responsive." He laughs, kissing my neck again briefly.

I blush, and they continue their conversation as my mind wanders about these guys. They clearly share girls a lot; they're so comfortable with each other. I continue to eat my food quietly until my plate is clear. A few minutes pass, and Levi starts clearing the plates while Devin brings his beer to my lips as I swallow. "Satisfied, baby?" he asks, and I shake my head.

"Not even a little."

Devin picks me up, placing me on the table. "Me either." He whispers, kissing me with no notice as his hands slip under my ass and start pulling down my thong. He puts it in his back pocket before he steps back, spreading my legs. "Fuck you have such a pretty pussy. How many guys have you been with?" he asks.

"Uh, three. All are ex-boyfriends."

"Damn, and they let this sweet thing go."

I go quiet, my mind going to Danny. Zane tilts my chin to him. "Whoever he is, forget him. He wasn't worth it. We're gonna make you forget him." I nod in response, not able to talk at this moment because I'm stuck between wanting to cry and letting it all go with these guys.

He pushes against my chest until I'm lying down on the table.

Levi runs the cold steel of his piercing over his lips, and I can't help but whimper, imagining what that feels like. Devin catches my reaction and nods to Levi, who replaces him between my thighs. "Now baby, Levi is gonna make you feel so good you're not even going to remember your own name, but I want you to focus on me and Zane, okay?" I nod, not really knowing what he means.

Levi pulls a chair up, sitting between my thighs before I feel his warm breath over my exposed clit. That's when I feel it. His cold piercing against my pussy lips as he licks all the way up before biting my clit. I squeal out, surprised, but God, it feels so good. Zane leans down, kissing me sensually as Levi works my pussy into a mess with his tongue, and I moan into Zane's mouth. Seeing stars behind my eyes. I feel my hand being grabbed as it's pulled to Devin's cock, Now realizing he stripped while Zane was kissing me. My fingers wrap around him as I start to stroke his very thick length. Fuck I don't know if I can take that, but I'm quickly distracted by Zane pulling my breast out of my bra and sucking on my already hard nipple.

This is...well, intense is an understatement.

Zane sucks on my nipple as Devin tweaks my other one rolling it between his fingers as I stroke his throbbing cock. Levi is still between my thighs, sucking and biting my clit playfully as he slips two fingers inside of me. "Oh God," I moan out.

"Not God, baby, he's definitely not here. You're with demons tonight," a voice says, but it's hard to figure out who said it.

I'm so overwhelmed. There are so many hands and mouths on my body I don't even know who is who anymore. Levi starts thrusting his fingers into my pussy so quickly that I feel my orgasm building. The room is filled with the sounds of us moaning and my pussy being so worked I can barely breathe.

Before I know what's happening, not only do I come, but I also squirt. I've never done that before, and I'm in shock. Levi chuckles, his face now buried in my pussy, licking every inch of my orgasm. My whole body trembles from the high before I feel my head being pulled to the side, and Devin captures my tongue with his. I vaguely hear Zane telling me how pretty I look as I come. Devin pulls back, and Levi walks over, taking his place so smoothly. Levi pulls me up the table so my head is hanging off it.

"Now, my pretty little slut. I want to hear you gag for me now that I've made you come for me."

Zane chuckles. "Breath through your nose, Goldilocks. Levi likes it to get rough."

CHAPTER FOUR

Fuck me, what is happening right now? I'm lying on the dining room table after just having the most intense orgasm of my life, my head hanging off as I watch Levi undress. His cock is now in his hand as he stands over me. I squeal as I feel a sharp slap against my sensitive pussy. The sound of Devin laughing fills my ears, but my eyes are focused on Levi right now. I open my mouth, and his fingers run across my tongue.

"Look at her, so eager and ready to please."

Well, I am, and the main reason is the silver piercing catching my attention through Levi's cock. He lowers himself down, and my tongue flicks out against his swollen balls. I hear him groan in pleasure, so I do it again before eagerly sucking on them as he strokes himself above me. Another slap to my pussy rings out, but this time I moan in ecstasy.

Fuck, why do I like that so much?

Zane is back sucking on my nipple, making me cry out in pleasure. I gasp, and Levi takes that exact moment to thrust his cock so deep in my mouth that I gag hard from the surprise. He keeps it there, his hand wrapping around my throat.

"That's it, baby, take it. Come on, I know you can do it."

I relax my throat, or at least try to, as he pushes his cock in deeper, but it only makes me gag harder as tears fall from my eyes.

"That's it, baby, gag on my cock." I feel saliva pour out of the side of my lips as I choke. *Fuck, fuck, fuck.* That's the only thought I have as I try to breathe through my nose, and before I know it, he removes his cock with such force I splutter, coughing as Zane pulls me up and smiles at me. His finger runs through a drop of my saliva that falls to my breast before he slips it back into my mouth, I still haven't caught my breath yet, but I suck on his digit eagerly. I want this. Is that wrong? I want to be treated and passed around them. It's already making me feel so wanted and desired…hell, even sexy.

Zane leans in, kissing me deeply. His fingers tease me between my thighs as I moan, letting my fingers weave into his and guide them lower. "Such a greedy little girl," he whispers against my lips. He lets me continue to guide him, and then he starts rubbing my clit in a circular motion, making me moan loudly into his mouth. "I want you in my bed, Goldilocks." He pulls his head back, looking at the boys, and they just grin back.

Devin smiles at me. "Well, she has broken into our cabin, eaten our food…"

"I didn't break in." I giggle.

"Ah, so you don't want to go to bed with us then…no?"

I pout. "I didn't say that." I gasp as Zane slips his fingers inside of me suddenly, curling them right at my G-spot.

"Hmmm, it does feel like you want it, but maybe you need to ask us…" he says.

"Beg us," Devin chimes in.

"I don't beg," I say, my eyes narrowing.

They all laugh at that, and before I know what's happening, I'm being picked up and thrown over Zane's shoulder as he spanks my ass hard. The sound rings out through the room, and I whimper in response. The sting of his hand on my ass burns a little, yet something in me wants him to do it again, so I push it.

"I don't beg!" I grit out.

Suddenly, I'm on my feet again. "Fine, guess we won't touch you then," Zane says as he and the boys chuckle. They all turn to walk upstairs, leaving me naked in the kitchen. Well that just blew up in my face.

"Wait… Where are you going?"

"Shower," Levi grunts before disappearing upstairs.

The other two nod. "Gotta take care of this, Goldilocks," Devin gestures down to his rock-hard cock throbbing in his hands as he tugs himself slowly. I find it hard to pull my eyes away.

"Just beg us and we will let you have every single inch of Devin and Levi and me. All at once if you crave it…"

I bite my lower lip, refusing to be broken this way. Devin shrugs, walking upstairs, leaving me alone with just Zane. "But…" he runs his finger over my lips, silencing me.

"No buts, no ifs. The only word we want to hear is please."

I shake my head, resolved that I'll never beg a guy to fuck me again. I did that with Danny at the end, and that's when things fell apart. He hadn't touched me in weeks, we barely spoke, and when I finally worked up the courage to confront him, well, that's when he finally came clean about the fact, he was shoving his dick in some slut called Megan. That's why he didn't want me. Zane's finger catches a tear that rolls down my cheeks as his face softens.

"Talk to me, Goldilocks." He guides me over to the sofa,

pulling me onto his lap. "Why are you crying? Because that fire inside of you wouldn't let you cry over us." I choke a sob down in reaction, trying to compose myself. My fingers dance over a tattoo he has on his chest. I didn't notice it before. "Blood in, no way out," I murmur to myself, reading it and looking up into his eyes curiously.

"Tell you what, you tell me why you're crying, and I'll tell you what this means."

I think that's a fair deal, so I spill my secrets. "My ex, Danny…we broke up last week. We were together since the first year of college. We were great, you know, the kind of couple everyone wants to be. He used to look after me and I him. Then, one day, we started to grow apart. I couldn't figure out why." I feel the tears flow freely.

"We stopped being…intimate." I blush softly, which is hilarious, considering we are both naked right now. "I begged him to touch me the night we broke up, begged him to let me back in, and that's when he told me. He didn't love me anymore. He was sleeping with one of my so-called friends and had been for about three months." I feel Zane tense underneath me.

Is he angry?

CHAPTER FIVE

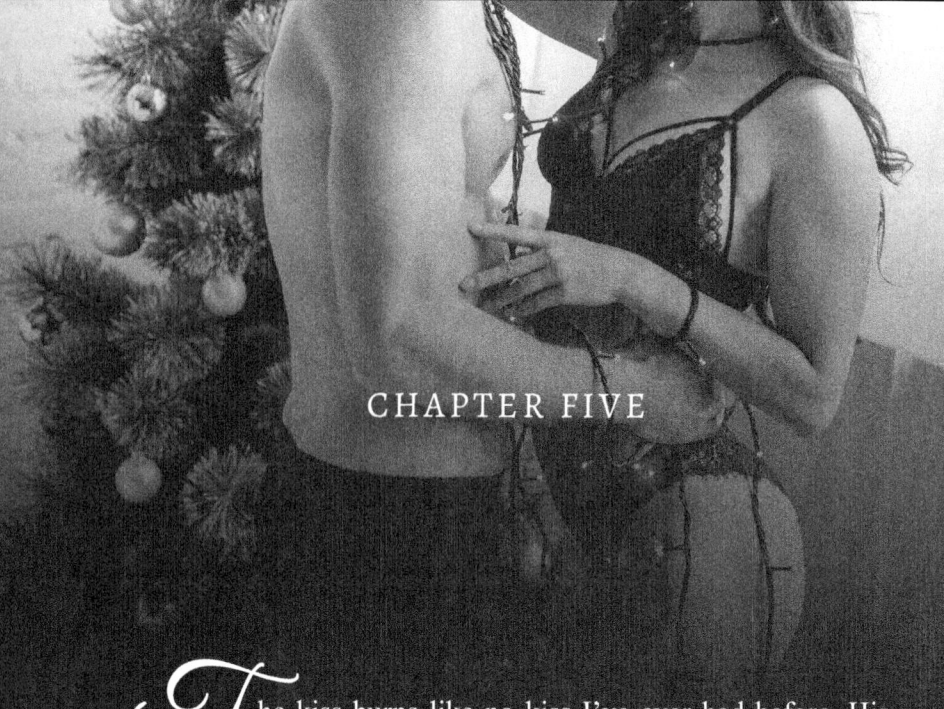

The kiss burns like no kiss I've ever had before. His hands grip my ass hard, squeezing each cheek so tightly they could bruise. He flips us suddenly, so I'm underneath him, lying on the couch. Before I even acknowledge what happened, he slams into me in one go, and sheer pain and pleasure erupt through my entire body as I cry out in ecstasy and a freedom I've never known before. "Oh god," I cry out loudly against his lips.

He chuckles, pushing my hair away from my face. "What did I tell you, beautiful? God has nothing to do with this." He resumes kissing me with him buried deep inside of me before he grabs my hands, pinning them above my head and propping himself up on his elbows.

"Focus on feeling me, on feeling that fire inside of you. Let it burn," he whispers. He pulls out nearly all the way before driving back in hard and fast, making me cry out as I feel my whole body tremble, wracked with pleasure I couldn't describe even if I wanted to.

I bite my lower lip as he pulls back out to the tip slowly.

"Feel it burn, Nova," he groans as he thrusts back into me so quickly I can't comprehend, even though I knew it was coming. I bite my lip harder, causing the skin to break and bleed. He notices and runs his thumb over the specks of blood on my lips, sucking on it slowly, and *holy fuck*, I've never seen anything sexier.

He leans down, kissing me again, the taste of my coppery blood on his tongue as he pulls back out before slamming into me again. I cry out his name against the kiss, and he smiles, kissing me even deeper.

"That's it, Nova," he whispers before letting go of my wrists. He pulls my left thigh up over his shoulder before he thrusts inside of me over and over again, fucking me within an inch of my life. His eyes never leave mine as I rake my nails down his back in a passion I can't describe. I know I've left marks, but he's leaving marks on me right now, ones I'll see and ones I won't, but I'll know they are there.

He fucks me with such ferocity I can't breathe; I can't understand what is happening. It's like an out-of-body experience watching everything that's happening to me yet feeling every single moment of it. He kisses my thigh before biting down on the skin, chuckling as I groan in response.

"Give me your fire. I want to feel it." He smiles down at me, and as my eyes meet his again, he grinds his cock inside of me, causing me to explode as I orgasm and give him exactly what he wants from me. He leans down, kissing me through my moment of ecstasy and bliss.

"I'm going to come soon, Nova. Where can I?" I look at him, confused for a second, until I realize he's asking my permission to empty himself inside of me.

I barely whisper, "Inside," as I bend my other leg up behind him, giving his ass a nudge as I smile wickedly at him. He kisses me one final time before he lets go, fucking me like an animal who wants to breed his mate. Over and over again until his eyes lock onto mine and I feel it. His warm sticky cum fills my pussy to a point I feel it spilling out of me. Running down my thighs. His head dips to my neck as he breathes my scent in. "Holy shit, Nova, you're something special," he says, barely breathing as he chuckles.

My fingers run through his hair before I tug on it, pulling his head up. "Thank you," I whisper, barely being able to breathe myself.

"You're welcome, Goldilocks."

"Damn, looks like I missed something here." I look over and see those honey-brown eyes looking at me. I smile at Devin, noticing his wet hair and his pale gray boxers with nothing else on.

"Mmm, just a bit." I giggle.

Zane chuckles as he slips out of me slowly, causing me to wince a little. "You have no idea yet…" he says to Devin, grinning in a way I know something is being schemed amongst them.

He jumps off me, and I watch as he slowly tugs his cock before walking to the kitchen and grabbing a beer. He takes a seat on the chair opposite me as Devin strolls over to me casually. He slips his fingers inside my swollen pussy, pulling a rope of Zane's cum from me before grinning. "Good girl." Then, I watch as his face delves into me before he aggressively eats my pussy, tasting his friend and my cum.

He pulls up, crawling over my body as I hear Zane say, "Open." I look between him and Devin, realizing what he means. I open my mouth, sticking my tongue out as Devin slowly drips the mess from his mouth into mine. Splattering on my tongue, coating my throat before he leans down and kisses me, devouring me and pushing the cum around in my mouth.

He pulls back slowly, biting my lip before he lets go and drops his fingers to my lips instead opening my mouth, making me show him the mess he made. "I wanted you to taste my friend princess, and now you need to taste me." He spits into my mouth so quickly I have to take a second.

Holy fuck.

Am I turned on by that?

I realize quickly I am, and I lie there rolling around our tastes in my mouth before blowing a bubble with it. I let it run down my chin as Devin takes his thumb, running it through it before putting it back into my mouth.

"Swallow," he orders me, and I do gladly, enjoying how we taste all mixed together. Devin smiles at me, pulling me up on his lap before kissing me slowly, sensually even, taking my breath away before he nudges me to the edge of the chair. He lies down next to me, wrapping his arms around my body and pulling me close.

CHAPTER SIX

We lie there for a few minutes, the three of us taking a moment of peace to get our breaths back.

"Are you guys…you know?" I ask shyly.

"Are we what?" Zane cocks his head, his ocean-blue eyes staring back at me with confusion.

"Gay?"

Devin starts laughing, pulling himself up as he pulls me up with him. "Why would you ask that?"

I blush. "You ate his cum out of me."

Zane laughs deeply. His cat-like frame shakes as he does.

Devin's hand goes to my chin, pulling it to face him.

"Not at all, Nova. I just wanted you to taste my friend, and I wanted to taste you."

I nod, blushing, feeling suddenly very naïve. Devin pulls me close so my head is resting against his chest as Levi finally comes downstairs. He's still naked, his thick cock swinging between his legs, and he looks like a dark naked god in all his glory walking through and into the kitchen. He comes back a few seconds later, handing us all a drink.

"She beg yet?"

I glare at him. "I don't beg."

Zane looks at him and gives him a small shake of his head, and Levi shrugs, walking over to my keyboard. "Come play something for me."

"I can't, I wouldn't know what to play." Devin gives me a nudge in encouragement, and I stand up before he spanks my ass. I look over at him, rolling my eyes before walking over to join Levi. I sigh as he pats the stool between his legs, and I take a seat, running my fingers lightly over the keyboard. My head cocks as I bite my lip and start playing a melody that's new to me. Something in me is inspired. Levi reaches over to my shoulder to my notebook, grabbing the pen too. I pause, looking down as he begins to write the notes I just played.

"How did you—"

He cuts me off. "I'm good with music." Is all he says, smirking. "Continue."

I sigh, carrying on. The notes are darker than what I have played before, deeper somehow, and I realize I'm writing a melody about the boys without realizing I was.

"What are you calling it?" Devin speaks, and I smirk at him.

"Depravity…"

They all laugh, and Levi pulls my hair back. "You have no idea what that means," he whispers in my ear.

"Then show me," I say, tipping my head back to him and leaning it against his chest.

He puts the notebook down, spreading my thighs over his knees. "Is that what you want, Goldilocks? To walk through that door?" I nod as my breath slows down.

His hand snakes up my body, caressing it slowly before it

sharply changes as he wraps his hand around my exposed throat and begins to squeeze.

"Do you know all the dark and depraved things I want to do to you, Nova?"

I shake my head as best I can after trying to speak, but no words cut out as he squeezes it tighter, cutting off my airways a little.

He smiles the most wicked smile I've ever seen before letting go of my throat. "You couldn't handle it." He tugs on my hair hard, making me squeal.

"I'm not so sure, Levi. I saw inside her earlier… She has a fire that could rival ours," Zane pipes up.

Levi scoffs in response. "Could rival ours, not does."

"Give me your best shot," I say in response, rubbing my neck a little.

He pushes me off his lap before moving the chair back. He grabs me, pulling me up as his hands slip under my ass, my legs wrapping around his waist as he does.

Where Zane and Devin kiss me with fire, Levi kisses me with ice, and it burns just as deeply. He backs me up against the wall, slamming my body into it. His hand wraps around my throat but not tight this time, just enough to hold me in place as he pulls back.

"Get it," he orders over his shoulder, and Devin pipes up, "I don't think that's a good idea, Levi…"

He chuckles, looking over at Devin. "I won't break her. She's not ready for that, and I don't think she ever will be, but she's just given me her permission to have some fun, and that's what I'm going to do." Devin exchanges a look between himself and Zane, and Zane gets up, walks upstairs, and comes back a minute later.

Levi has been staring at me intensely, just smirking.

Something in me is terrified right now, but not for what he could do or could mean. I know he won't hurt me, not in that way, but I'm terrified of exposing myself to him in a way so completely I could end up showing him a part of myself I'm not ready to.

I look at Zane as he reappears, and he's holding a knife in his hand, and when I say a knife, I mean some scary ass blade.

What the actual fuck is happening?

He flips it in his hand so he's holding the blade side before Levi drops me on my feet, his hand still around my throat before he grabs the knife by the handle from Devin. "Open up my little perfect slut…I need you to get this all wet and sloppy." I swallow hard before opening my mouth for him.

Zane leans against the wall, watching us with bated breath. I think he's surprised I opened my mouth. Levi slips the handle in my mouth. "Suck on it, suck on it like you did my cock earlier." I do as he asks, bobbing my head up and down as he starts fucking my mouth with it.

The room is silent except for the gagging sounds I'm making as he pushes it further and further, making my saliva and drool run down my chin. "You're such a perfect little whore for me, aren't you, Nova?" I can't talk or nod as he holds me by my throat, pinning me against the wall. All I can do is moan in response.

He lets go of me, "Go lay on the chair again, Nova… Sit in Devin's lap." I gasp as he lets go, pulling the knife from my throat. I obey, walking over to Devin as he lazily smiles at me, patting his leg, and I take a seat on his lap. Devin pulls me down slightly, spreading my legs wide in a split as I look up at him. He smirks, kissing me deeply as I feel Levi thrust his fingers inside my soaked pussy.

"So ready for me already." Devin stops the kiss as Levi pulls his fingers from me, sticking them down my throat, making me cough and splutter. "This knife…I sleep with it… It's the knife I used to kill my own father. I'm sentimental that way." He smirks. "I've used it since then, several times, in fact. I've carved my initials into girls' bodies before, Nova. They begged me to; they wanted to be owned by me, owned by my blade. I'm not going to do that to you, though, but I am going to slip it into this tight little pussy, and I want you to hold it in while Devin plays with you." My eyes widen in shock. His eyes are almost black. "Still want my depravity, Nova? You can say no now… back out while you can."

I shake my head, and he sighs. "I knew it. I knew you couldn't handle it."

"I'm not saying no. I'm telling you I'm not backing out. Show me"—reaching out to his hand that holds the blade—"do it."

The voice that leaves me isn't a voice I recognize. This girl sounds confident and fearless.

He leans in, kissing me slowly as he slides the handle into me. It's uncomfortable at first, but I know it's meant to be. This isn't something that should be done, yet it almost seems natural.

I squeeze internally, holding the knife inside of me. I gasp as I squeeze my legs together and feel how sharp the exposed blade is as it touches my thighs. "Uh uh, Goldilocks, the idea isn't to watch you bleed," Devin whispers, pulling my legs back open. "You're going to have to do it," he says to Levi, "I don't trust she won't try and squirm."

Zane walks over, takes a seat next to Devin, and holds one of my thighs hard, almost bruising, as he nods at Levi. Devin holds my other one just as tightly as he kisses me. "Keep squeezing, beautiful, or Levi will stop."

I look back at Levi as he tugs his cock. He looks back at me with such intensity it's almost frightening. The silver piercing glints in the light. I squeeze my core hard, feeling the knife pulling itself deeper inside of me, gasping when it grazes against my G-spot.

Levi smiles at me, and something in me is proud of myself in this moment. He gets on his knees between my thighs and blows on my clit, my hands go into his hair, and he chuckles.

"That's it, pull on my hair, baby," he whispers before he sucks my clit in between his lips. Devin tips my head to his side to kiss me as Zane takes my nipple between his teeth and bites it playfully. My hand continues to tug on Levi's hair.

The feeling of having three guys doting on me at the same time is insane. I feel Levi suck, bite, lick my clit, devouring it as I try to keep the handle of the blade inside of me. It only builds an intense feeling inside of me. Freedom, that's how it feels. I'm discovering myself here with these guys, discovering how deep into madness I can go. Levi's thumb teases my asshole, and I immediately tense.

Levi chuckles, "Never been taken here, baby?" Devin chuckles, breaking the kiss. I shake my head no. He just nods, slowly stroking over my hole. "What a shame we don't have time to train you to take one of us here." He uses his hand to twist the blade inside of me, and I gasp in ecstasy as Zane pulls my hand to his cock, now out and proud again as I remember how he felt inside of me.

Devin pulls his cock out and smiles at me. "Taste me," he whispers, and Levi pulls the blade out and steps back. I get on my hands and knees on the couch as Zane moves closer to Devin. My hand goes to his cock as my mouth lowers over Devin's, taking him whole. Levi repositions himself behind us and starts slipping his knife back into my pussy. Fucking me with it slowly as I suck his friend's cock. Devin's hands go to my hair, pulling it into a ponytail.

"You can do better than that, Goldilocks." He pushes my head down on his cock, and I gag hard, my saliva dripping down over his shaft and his balls.

Fuck, this turns me on so much. I feel needed, sexy, desired —a feeling I lost after Danny. Levi pushes the blade in as far as the handle will go. I feel something wet around my asshole as I realize Levi just spit on it, and then I gasp as I feel his thumb slip in just a little. "Hold it in," he whispers as I feel the blade slipping out of me.

My hand continues moving up and down on Zane's cock as I try to squeeze my pussy to stop the knife from slipping any further. Devin starts pulling on my hair, lifting me up a little as he thrusts into my mouth. The room fills with glugging sounds as Devin fucks my mouth and throat.

I gasp as he rips me off, kissing me deeply. "I want her pussy" He orders out loud, and I realize in this moment Devin's cool act is a front. They may all be brothers, but clearly, he's in charge of the trio.

Levi laughs, slipping his thumb further into my tight asshole, making me moan in ecstasy. He pulls out the blade from my pussy, and I sigh in pleasure as he does. He moves his thumb slowly out of me. "Fine," he says, and I can tell he's a little disappointed that Devin won't let it go any further.

CHAPTER SEVEN

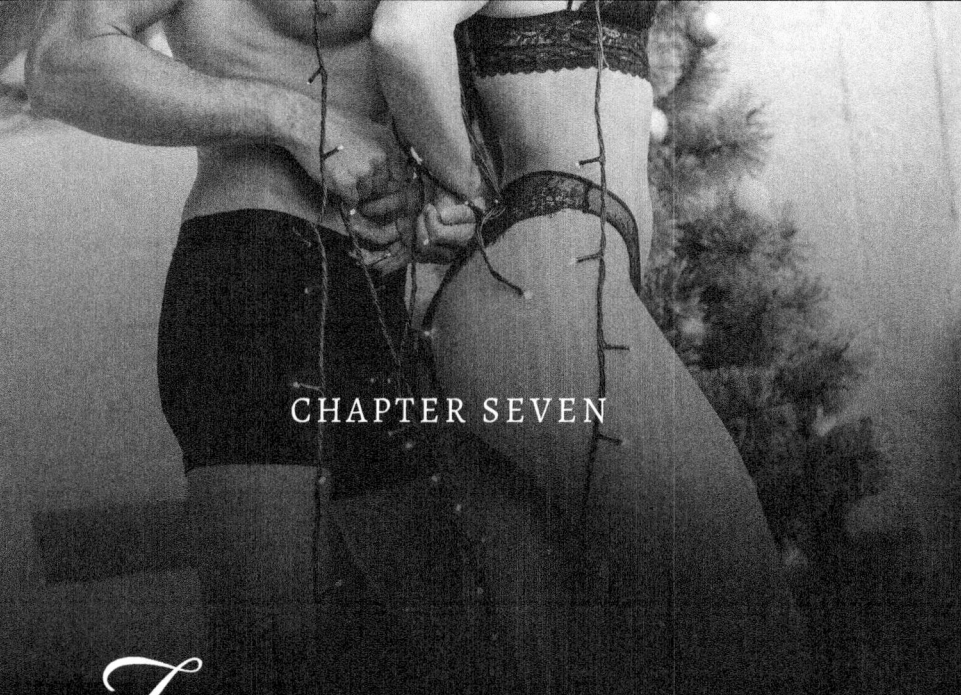

Zade moves from under me, and Devin sits me upright before taking my hand. "Not here, Goldilocks. I want to make you scream in my bed." He picks me up, and I wrap my legs around him, staring into his eyes as he stares just as intensely back.

He walks us up the stairs, and the guys go to follow, but he looks back at them. "I want twenty minutes alone with her first." I look at him curiously. He didn't seem to have any problem with the boys sharing me before. I pout, and he laughs. "Don't worry, Nova, they will be up soon." He continues to walk us up the stairs, walking along a hallway before kicking what I assume is his bedroom door.

He walks in, dropping me on the bed, and I take a moment to look at him. God, he is a fine specimen of a man. Tall and broad, abs I just want to lick, and a cock glistening with my saliva standing to order.

"Eyes up here, Nova." I blush as I pull my eyes from his throbbing cock to his eyes staring at me. "How much do you trust me? Trust us?"

I pause for a second, unsure how to answer. I just met these guys, yet I've let them fuck me, use my mouth, play with me, and more. I don't know why, but I do trust them. I nod my head. "I trust you."

He smiles, petting my hair and cupping my chin to make my head go higher to look at him. "I'm going to tie you up, Nova, and it's not exactly going to be comfortable for you. But I promise it will feel good, and you're safe with me, with us, okay?" He slips his thumb between my lips, and I nod as I suck on it gently. "Good girl," he whispers, leaning down to kiss me on the forehead. He walks over to his dresser, pulling out solid black handcuffs and four long pieces of black silky fabric. I whimper softly, and he smiles at me, proud of my reaction.

"I want you to get on your hands and knees for me, Nova. Face the head of the bed."

I do as he asks, and he pulls my hands behind my back with such ferocity I nearly fall. He locks the cuffs around my wrists. "Too tight?" he asks, and I shake my head in response as he clicks them tighter.

"Ow."

He laughs, whispering in my ear, "Good girl," and I feel like putty in his hands.

He pulls my legs together, tying them up with one of the long pieces of fabric. He pushes my back down so my head rests against the bedspread. "Fuck you look delicious like this." The next silk scarf goes around my lips like a gag as he ties it behind my head. Fuck, this could get dangerous, but a voice in me tells me that Devin meant it when he said I was safe with him.

The next tie goes around my eyes, blinding me. I can't see or speak now. I'm completely and utterly powerless, yet that thrills me to hand over that control and the ownership of my body to someone else. "You wanted dark and depraved," he whispers in my ear, and it makes me jump. He pulls my stomach back so I'm sitting on my legs that are folded under me. His lips go to my shoulder as he kisses it, his fingers swirling around my stomach.

"If you were mine, if you were truly ours forever, I would breed you over and over again. But you're not, and this is one night."

I sigh in pleasure. Having my senses taken away only heightens his words, the low tone in his voice, the touch on my stomach.

"Fuck me, Nova… You have no idea how tempted I am to keep you, lock you away, and never have any man look at you again except us."

I go to say something to bite back, but I can't, and he laughs in response.

"Don't worry, I won't. You have other houses to break into, Goldilocks. But what I and my brothers are going to do is fuck you into a moaning mess, and you're going to take it, every time, every inch, even after your body is exhausted and your eyes are heavy with sleep. You are ours tonight, do you hear me?" I nod, unable to speak to even form a thought. "You wanted depraved, remember? Well, Nova…what you have seen is just a tiny little peek into how depraved and dark we can be."

I hear a door open and footsteps on the wooden floor. It's my other demons, my head cocks to the side to follow the sound. I hear them both laugh.

"Well, doesn't Goldilocks look delicious enough to eat and fuck and use like a good little slut!" I know that's Levi, and God do I want him to do all of that to me. Something about Levi calls to me; they all do. I feel my head being pulled and a kiss laid against my cheek.

"Hey, Goldilocks, you know you're locked in a house with three big bad men, and you, my girl, are utterly under our mercy. I nod softly against the gag, wishing they would just touch me.

I feel a hand go around my throat, squeezing just enough to show me who is in control here, my gag being pulled down before a warm tongue slips into my mouth. There's no tongue piercing, so I know it's not Levi. Devin is still holding my stomach, so it must be Zane. His kisses take my breath away anyway, but his hold around my throat tightens even more. He lets go pulling back, and I feel myself being pushed down on the bed before a hard cock slips between my pussy lips, guiding its way up and down, teasing me. I feel the bed dip, and something warm brushes against my lips. "Open, my beautiful little slut."

It's Levi, and my mouth opens wide eager to take his thick cock between my lips. He thrusts up straight away, making me gag and drool over his hard dick. He chuckles. "That's it, beautiful," he whispers. "You look so pretty like this."

I slide my mouth down, and just as I hit the base of his cock, Devin slides into my soaked pussy, and I gasp in ecstasy. This man is thick. I can feel him stretching me, and my breath catches, which only pulls Levi's cock deeper.

I wish I could explain this moment in better words, but I can't. It's overwhelming, to say the least. Devin drives his cock slowly but deeply, thrusting hard as he pulls nearly all the way back. A loud smack rings through the air, and I realize I've been spanked once, twice, three times. There's pain in these boys' pleasure, but it only heightens every feeling. I wonder for a moment where and what Zane is doing. But it lasts only a moment as Levi's hands go around my head as he relentlessly starts fucking my throat at the same time as Devin starts driving hard and fast into me fucking me mercilessly.

"Fuck, this pussy. Nova, you're strangling my dick, I swear." I whimper, my saliva running down Levi's shaft. These boys are something else. What, I don't know. They called themselves demons earlier, but the pleasure they bring to my body, I know they can't be really. Could someone that damned bring this much ecstasy.

Levi lets go of my hair to bring me up as he spits into my mouth before kissing me so desperately. I hear a whisper in my ear—Zane. "Such a good girl for us, aren't you, Nova?" I moan into Levi's mouth. I swear these guy's dirty talk could make me orgasm all on its own. Zane starts sucking on my earlobe before Devin starts to groan. His cock pumps harder and faster before coming to a slow as I feel warm heat fill me, and I realize he's just come inside of me.

"Fuck" I hear, followed by a chuckle before I feel another hard slap to my ass. "So damn good."

He pulls out slowly, and I feel his cum drip out of my pussy and down my thighs. Long fingers push inside of my pussy as he scoops his cum out of me. "Take off her mask," Devin orders, and Levi stops the kiss to do as he says. I'm spun around quickly, Levi pulling me to his chest to sit over him. Zade pulls the silk ties around my legs, undoing them so my legs straddle either side of Levi before he impales me with his long length.

I gasp at the sudden shock before Devin shoves his cum-covered fingers into my mouth. "Suck on them, Nova, just like you did Levi's cock. Show me what a good little slut you are."

I suck eagerly, just like I did with Levi's length wanting to taste Devin and I do. Hot, salty cum is pushed down my throat as I gag on his fingers. I taste my own pussy on them too. "God, do you know how beautiful you look with these tears down your face," he says as he wipes them away so softly. I nod as he keeps his fingers in my mouth.

I start to bounce hard on Levi's cock, and I hear him groan as I take his length inside of me. "You want another cock, princess?" Zane asks, and I smile over Devin's fingers, nodding eagerly just like they want. Like I want.

Devin moves to the side, his fingers going to my clit as I cry out. Zane pulls my hair to the side as he stands above me on the bed, his cock level with my mouth, and I lean forward as I start to pump his cock between my lips. I must be dreaming. Moments pass before I feel my orgasm hit, and I come. My eyes roll back as Levi continues to fuck me into oblivion. He thrusts, knowing I'm coming, and Zane just smiles down at me, taking control as he thrusts slowly into my mouth.

"Good fucking girl," I hear Levi say before I feel him empty himself inside of me. "Good. Fucking. Girl." He groans, pulling my hips down against him as he drives into me a final time.

A few more seconds of Zane thrusting into my mouth, and warm salty cum shoots down my throat. I want to take every drop, but there's so much I gag as it spills out between my lips. And down my chin.

Zane looks at me, slowly pulling out. His thumb runs through a rope of cum spilling down my chin before he slips it into my mouth. "You, Nova, are close to perfection." He cups my face and kisses me slowly, sensually, as I sigh. My eyes heavy.

He pulls back slowly, and I miss the taste of his tongue. But I'm too exhausted to protest.

Devin slowly pulls me off Levi and guides me between him and Levi, laying me down on the bed.

"Sleep, Goldilocks," he whispers, pulling a stray hair away from my face. I want to protest; I want more, but nothing comes as I drift into a heavenly unconsciousness.

CHAPTER EIGHT

I'm woken in what I assume is a few hours later by a cock pressed inside of my pussy. I open my eyes, and it's Levi. The other guys are asleep next to me. His hand quickly goes to my throat, squeezing tightly so I can barely breathe, let alone talk. He goes slow, still hard and deep, but so agonizingly slow. He squeezes that little bit harder, making me see stars as my vision starts to blur. He leans down, kissing me slowly, almost sensually. It's a strange combination, a soft kiss while this man chokes me to nearly unconsciousness. He lets go of my throat just as I feel myself slipping, pulling away from my lips as he smiles at me. Fingers touch my cheek and pull my head to the side, and it's Devin.

"Naughty girl, having fun without us." He leans forward, kissing me just as sensually as Levi did as he continues to thrust in slowly and then drag himself out again.

I tilt my head back to Levi as I look up at him. My fingers reach out, pushing his hair from his eyes as they glint at me in the dark.

"Show me," I whisper to him as Zane begins to stir. I see

him look at Devin, and he looks back intensely. He tilts my head back to me.

"Are you sure, Nova? If you let Levi go there, it's permanent. You can't rewind this, you can't erase it."

"I know, but I want it."

Levi slides out of me as Devin shifts. Levi pulls the ties from earlier before flipping me over to my stomach. He doesn't speak, doesn't make a sound. He pulls my hands behind me as Devin grabs my legs up. I realize I'm being hogtied together. Levi walks to a nearby dresser and pulls something from it, but I can't see what it is. But then I feel cool leather being wrapped around my neck. Suddenly, it's pulled, and I realize he's collared me and it's attached to a leash. He pulls my neck back so I'm looking up. Fuck this is uncomfortable. I feel something pull behind me, and I notice he's tied the leash to the hogtie so I'm now stuck in this position.

Zane, who is now awake, sits up on the bed, watching in silence, his eyes sparkling as he realizes I've truly submitted to them. I watch him stroke his cock, tugging on his length as it gets harder and more swollen.

Levi moves around to me, his knife shining in the moonlight that's pouring through the window.

"We're all going to fuck you now, it's going to be rough and uncomfortable with you like this. Do you understand?"

"Yes," I say sincerely, looking into those near-black eyes.

"We're not going to care about your pleasure, do you understand?"

"Yes."

"We're each going to come, but we choose where. Do you understand?"

"Yes."

"Nova, you are not allowed to come till we say, do you understand?"

"Yes," I say breathlessly, his words shaking me to my core in the best possible way.

"After Nova, I'm going to cut you. It's going to bleed a little, but it won't cause damage, I'll make sure you're looked after. Do you understand?"

I take a beat. "Yes."

"Good girl. Now, this is important. Really listen to me. If at any point you want us to stop, you have to say something. Pick a word now, something you wouldn't usually say."

"Banana"

He smirks, nearly laughing, "Banana?"

"Well, I hate them, so I wouldn't usually say that word…"

"Banana it is… now there may be times where you can't use your mouth. Can you cross your fingers for me?"

I do it easily as my fingers are not restricted.

"Good girl, if you can't speak, you cross your fingers, understand? We will stop immediately."

"Yes, I understand."

He leans in kissing me slowly, I know how much this means to him, to all of them. And I'm glad I can give it to them.

"Good girl," he whispers before pulling back and walking away.

Devin pulls me up slightly as Zane slips pillows under my stomach to prop me up.

CHAPTER NINE

*D*evin looks down at me from behind. "Open your mouth for me, beautiful." I do, slipping my tongue out. His fingers caress my jaw and chin as he leans down, letting a long line of spit drop into my mouth. "Don't you dare swallow that till I'm through with you."

I close my mouth, rolling it around, tasting him as he spanks my ass hard, leaving his handprint behind, I'm sure. He does it again, the other cheek this time before I feel his thickness start to stretch me. His hand goes to where my hands are tied, gripping it tightly, pulling my neck further back so I can do nothing but looks at him as he begins to pound into my pussy.

Over and over again, I can do nothing but take it. Is it uncomfortable? Rough? Yes, but do I love it? Double yes. I already feel my orgasm building, but I know Levi's rules. I try to not think of it, but as Devin thrusts against my G-spot repeatedly, it's hard to not think about the pleasure he's giving me. Levi runs his knife lightly down my arm from the side of me. The cold metal versus the hot intensity of this fuck drives me wild. I'm not the girl everything thinks I am, after all.

He continues to pound, to take everything from me, occasionally spanking my ass hard over and over again before I feel him pull out of me as his hot sticky cum sprays over my ass, almost cooling the sting I still feel from his hands. Fuck I've never let a guy come all over me. Yet, here I am, being completely submissive, completely under their spell and control.

He leans down and says, "Open, baby," and I do as he asks and show him I'm still holding his spit in my mouth. Just as I do, he shoves his cock in. "Clean me up," he orders as he slowly fucks my mouth, his spit being pushed down my throat. He then leans down, pinching my nose so I can't breathe as he pushes further down my throat. Tears fall from my eyes as I struggle to take his thick shaft, yet I thrive in it, revel in this loss of control.

Before I have a chance to think, I feel Levi's cock slide deep inside of me. "Such a pretty little slut covered in cum, aren't you, Nova." I moan, trying to agree, yet it just pulls Devin's cock deeper. He finally lets go, pulling his cock from my mouth and letting go of my nose. As he steps back, seemingly proud of me, I gasp for air.

Levi slides in and out of me slowly, hitting my G-spot every time. Long, slow thrusts, making sure I feel every inch of him before his thumb starts playing with my other hole again. "You have no idea how badly I want this…it's like you're giving me one long tease." He pulls out, moving around and fucking my mouth again. "You want my cum down your pretty throat, Nova?" I nod as best I can feeling in a way I can't describe, I feel desired, wanted, needed. Most girls would find this degrading, yet it makes me feel powerful.

"Then suck, my pretty little whore" I start sucking his cock, pumping it as best I can in this position as I feel Zane move around me. He strums my clit, making me moan as Levi whispers, "Remember, you can't come." Zane chuckles behind me. *Asshole.*

He slips inside of me, holding me by my neck as Levi pumps himself down my throat, slowly teasing me with the taste of him but not letting me have it just yet. Zane fucks me with ferocity as his spare hand palms my clit with his fingers. Everything is so intense, so freeing.

Zane leans down, whispering in my ear as he hits so deep my body tenses. "There's that fire. Now come for me, Goldilocks," he says before I feel him empty himself inside of me fully, just as Levi spills down my throat. The sensation makes me orgasm almost instantly, and I swear I black out.

They both hold me for a moment before they finally pull out. Devin takes time to untie me gently, knowing my wrists are hurting. He kisses each one sweetly as I lay on the bed, exhausted once more. Before he turns me over, kissing me sweetly. "You did so good, Goldilocks."

Levi sits on the bed. "Where do you want it?" he asks.

It takes me a moment to realize he's talking about his blade. Fuck I don't know. There's a little shiver of terror running down my spine.

"If you want, you can say it. Say your word."

I shake my head. "You choose," I whisper in response, barely able to talk. Devin and Zane pull me close to them and as I lay in their arms, Levi tips my body slightly so my hip is exposed to him.

Then I feel the sharp steel of the blade pierce my flesh. It hurts but not so bad I want to scream.

He leans down, licking the blood clean before looking at

me. "What do you think baby?" I look down and see he's cut a small star. It's not deep; if anything, it's kinda beautiful. I pull myself from the arms of the guys, kissing Levi slowly and briefly. "I love it."

CHAPTER TEN

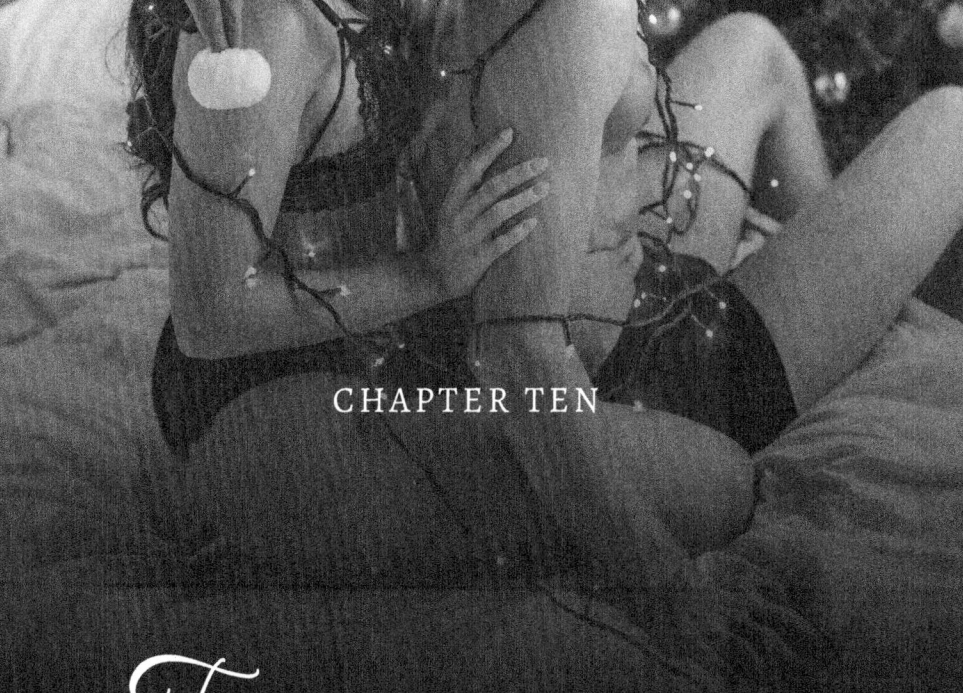

The following day goes by in a blur. I wake up in Levi and Zane's arms. The guys spent hours last night caring for me. They put me in the bath, cleaning their mess from me. We then spent hours in bed hugging and kissing before we all fell asleep wrapped up in each other. For a second, I giggle to myself, just taking in the events of last night before Zane awoke to my laughing and proceeded to tickle me. Devin made breakfast for us as we sat together, basking in the pleasure still running through our veins, and here I am now, standing at my car as the boys start packing my stuff into it.

The snow cleared, and Devin brought his car in from the road, making sure it was safe for me to drive in. The blizzard is long gone now. I never thought I would be so thankful for a snowstorm.

Levi walks over, wrapping a piece of tinsel from the tree around my neck before he picks me up, hugging me tightly. "Something to remember us by. Look after yourself, Nova, and make sure you finish that song. I'm pretty sure you have a ton of inspiration now."

I laugh, punching him in his arm as he places me down on the ground. I look up at Zane, and he grins that cheeky cat-like smile at me. "So, what was his name again?"

I smile back. "I don't remember… I only remember three guys' names right now."

He chuckles in response nodding before bringing me into a hug against his chest as he kisses the top of my hair. "Good girl." Levi immediately wraps his arms back around me and I shake my head laughing. Me and Levi shared something last night. We gave each other a piece of ourselves, and I'll never forget that.

Devin puts my last bag in the trunk, closing it. I take a step out of Levi's arms and look up at the honey-gold eyes that make my heart race for what I think may be the last time.

"No more breaking into strange men's houses, got it, Goldilocks?" A smirk dances over his lips.

"Hmmm, as long as you promise not to corrupt any more girls you find sleeping on your couch." He laughs outrageously before picking me up. His hands scoop under my thighs as he walks and presses me into the trunk of my car, devouring me with a kiss that makes me wonder if I will see him again after all. He tucks my hair behind my ear sweetly. "No promises, gorgeous." I laugh before he backs away, letting me slide to my feet.

"Thank you," I say to all of them. They all know what I mean. I really don't need to say anything more.

Devin smirks, "Trust me, it was our pleasure. Look us up if you're ever in…"

I shake my head, cutting him off, not wanting to know and ruin this moment with what ifs, walking to the side of my car and getting in. I start the ignition, taking one final look in my mirror at the boys before I drive away, lyrics dancing through my mind about a weekend I will never forget.

EPILOGUE

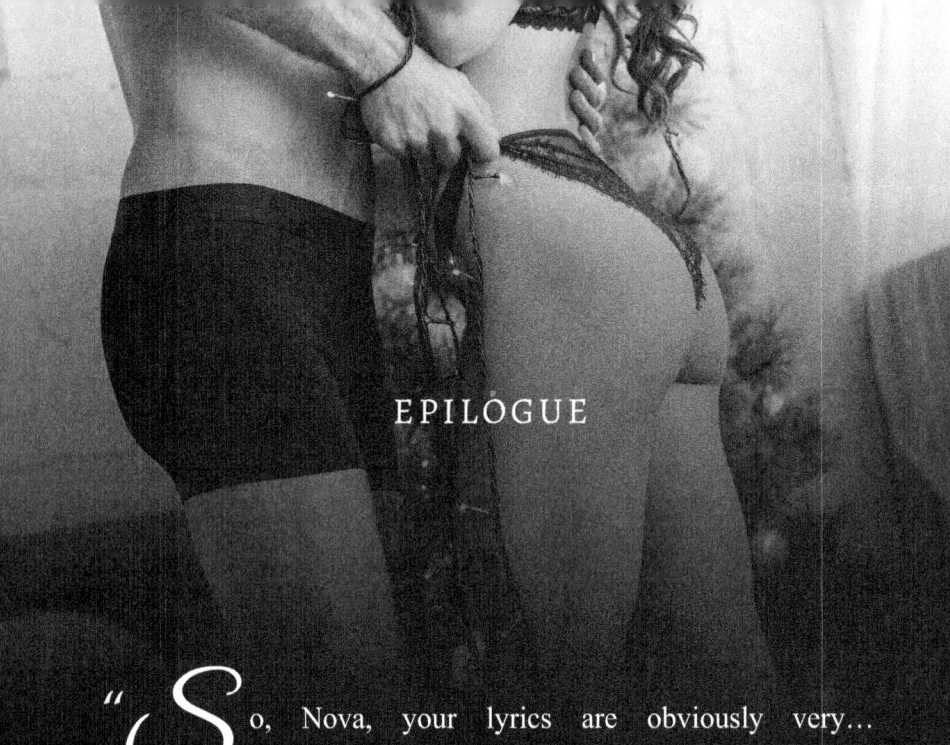

"So, Nova, your lyrics are obviously very... provocative." She giggles lightly, and I smile back innocently. "I think we're all hoping there is some filthy, sordid story behind them. I mean, the thing everyone wants to know is this—where does your inspiration come from? The song One Weekend with The Devils—did that really happen?"

I run my tongue over my lips, slowly biting my lower one before leaning forward. "You want to know a secret?" I ask her before winking at the camera. "Okay, here it is." I curl my finger at the camera as I know he's zooming in as I speak.

"My music is for all the girls that seek excitement, crave a little bit of bad in their lives. Go find your devils, go find your depravity and danger. I know I did." I wink to the camera and then someone calls time.

I look over at Millie before she smiles, shaking my hand and thanking me for the time. I smile politely in response before my phone starts buzzing. It's a FaceTime call from a number I don't recognize. I answer cautiously, wondering who it is. The phone pings as a video pops up of one of my demons playing with his tongue piercing.

"Hey, Goldilocks."

I smile, shaking my head. "How did you get my number?" I ask, surprised.

Zane pulls the phone away from his as Levi tells him off. "Ah, see, that's for your devils to know and you to dot dot dot." I laugh as he uses my own words against me from when they asked me about my kinks.

"Give me the phone," Devin says, pulling the phone to face him.

"I'm proud of you, Nova, we just watched your clip online live. Had to keep an eye on whether you're breaking into anyone else's houses."

I roll my eyes. "I promise I'm definitely not being good."

I hear a massive cheer, and Zane shouts out, "Damn, she's an animal." I realize they're at the club they talked about

"I gotta go, Nova. We got a new fighter in, and she's a wildcat. I think we might need to get her out before she kills someone. Hey, look us up when you're in Asheville. I can see you're playing at a club local to us in a couple of months. You have Levi's number now; don't be a stranger."

"Definitely—go tame that wildcat," I say, laughing with no jealousy in me at all, knowing I had these boys for a weekend, and that was enough for me. We don't fit into each other's worlds, but I am so thankful for them showing me who I truly am.

Devin gives me a wink before hanging up. I smile, walking back to the dressing room and packing up my things as I toy with the idea of looking them all up in the new year. I touch the charm that I made on my bracelet. It's a clear glass ball that has a single thread of tinsel in it. A piece from the one that Levi gave me.

Maybe I could exist in their world for one more night…

AUTHOR NOTE

Hey guys, my name is Melody Mode. I started this journey into the book world as a reader, just like you. I devoured thousands of books over the years, but I couldn't shift the voices in my head. Most people would think I'm crazy for saying that, but I promise, the voices aren't telling me to kill, though some of them are killers. I realised it was my characters wanting to be heard, so I sat down one day, and hours later, I realised I had started to write my own book.

Before I knew it, I was published, and it's been a crazy ride since. I want to thank you all for reading my novella about The Twisted Brothers. They will be getting their own books in 2024, but if you want to meet more of our sinners in Asheville, check out A Touch of Heaven, part of the Unholy Bastards series. You get to meet Chase, Asher, and Jax, who were mentioned in this book.

Don't forget to come find me on social media and let me know your thoughts, or just drop by for a chat.

Drop by my group Melody Mode's Raunchy Readers on Facebook or look me up on Instagram and TikTok.

Now, just before I give you a little tease of my book, A Touch of Heaven, I want to thank everyone who read this book and took a chance on a baby author. Also, a huge thank you to my PA, Cassie Weaver, who puts up with a hell of a lot from me. Thank you to all my teams for your support, and lastly, a small thank you to my fellow Reverse Harem authors. You helped me find a trope I didn't know I needed as a reader. You truly inspire me and give me a space to find myself, without you I never could have been so delightfully sinful.

Without Further Ado… Let me introduce you to The Unholy Bastards.

PROLOGUE

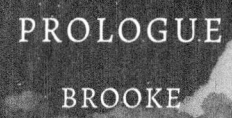

BROOKE

I wish I could say my life was black. At least black has some substance to it, some depth. At the very least, it gives an emotion, a feeling, something behind the darkness. A hope that life could get better and change in some way. You just have to see the light.

But it would be wrong to describe my life like that. My life was gray. Gray is the absence of color. It's just so…so…blah. I mean, take the gray and add any color; all you get is more gray. It's nothing. It's boring, uneventful, an empty space. Yep, my life was gray. That was until he came and changed it.

Like a world to his own, he entered my life, my safe space and he took everything from me, stripped away all I was until it was just him. Those intense eyes bare down on me, thrilling me to the darkest depths of my soul. I always feel like I am drowning in them, but I didn't know what that was like until tonight.

I used to think it was an amazing feeling, but drowning in someone is frightening, heartbreaking, and just simply tragic.

You lose all ability to think clearly, you can't breathe, you can't make decisions, and your body and mind just shut down on themselves.

When he used to look at me, it felt like he was breathing air into my lungs, but now it's different. I always knew he would take me to new heights of pleasure. What I didn't realize was that he would show me real pain, too.

That voice that carried hate and bitterness also carried lust, passion, and love. He turned my life into colors.

I was blinded by it.

Naïve.

I just didn't realize the color I would be left with was blood red and that it would stain my soul. I knew from the moment he revealed his secret I would stand by him and watch him burn the world. I would stand and watch the ashes fall to the ground and bury anyone who stood in our way. I never realized the fire burning the world down around us would catch and harm the people I love.

This summer was meant to be the best summer of my life. I was spending it with my best friends and the man I had loved since I was five. He was meant to be my prince charming, my happily ever after.

Instead, my entire world crumbled around me. My own selfishness and idiocy are the reasons I'm covered in blood and losing the one person in my life who loved me more than they do anyone or anything else.

"Please don't leave me," I plead, sobbing as his blood soaks my shirt like spilled juice. It's hot and surprisingly sticky. It's a funny thought to have as he lays there dying in my arms, what his blood feels like. My tears fall on his face as I hold him in my arms, rocking him to me. The pit in my stomach grows every moment as I look at him.

This is all my fault. I should have taken the chance I had while I still could have.

"I can't do this without you," I choke out.

He raises his hand and caresses my cheek. His touch is cold against my warm skin in the hot night air, and that's not how it should be. His touch is usually hot, caring, and sweet, but this is wrong. So, fucking wrong. His touch usually makes me feel safe and loved, but now it does nothing to chase my cares or fears away.

"Please, why won't anyone help?" I scream at those around me.

This has to be a dream; I need to wake up.

Why won't I wake up?

They all stand there watching. They're not doing anything. I hear someone scream, and I watch her fall to her knees. I'll never forget that scream. That will haunt me until the day I die. It's harrowing, the one you hear and know there's no point in trying. You can feel the pain, the loss, the torment, and I know no one will help because there's nothing we can do.

This is it. I look over at my friend on her knees; she knows the same as me. I look at her—broken, crying as her dark angel holds her. This isn't real. She's not like this. She's always so strong, the one that faces the world and screams at it, but now she's just as damaged as me.

"Baby," I look down at his face, that gorgeous face that always makes me feel safe and loved. "Please don't go, don't do this, you're going to be okay, just hold on, please," I plead with him as if begging will do anything against this heartless act.

He smiles softly, "I'm sorry for what I said, Brooke. I love you."

My tear lands on his cheek. "I love you too," I whisper, "so you have to stay with me, okay?"

He spits blood out of his mouth, and it runs down his chin. I try desperately to wipe it away. I can hear him gagging on it as it fills his lungs. His hand drops from my face with a sudden thud to the ground, so deafening I will never forget it.

That will be the last sound I ever hear from him. Not his laugh, not my name on his lips, not him poking fun at me or trying to make me feel better. Just a loud, dull thud of his hand as it lands in the sand around us.

I can hear the sirens in the background. Help is coming, but it's too late. You're meant to hear those and feel hope, but my hope just died along with the only one who loved me so purely and without fault.

I'm done being the innocent princess. I'm done being that naïve little girl. I can feel the cold seep in, taking root deep inside me, making me its new home. Like the blood seeping into my jeans, this cold seeps into my soul, my very being, every little crack. I gently slip my hands from around him, leaving him on the ground.

I don't get up. I don't think my feet would hold me if I tried. Instead, I embrace the cold and darkness and pray it makes me numb for what I need to do. I feel arms pull me up off the ground, locking me in their embrace as they pull me to their chest to look away. They expect me to break down, to sob, but the tears stop coming. There's nothing left inside of me. I just look at him on the ground. He's gone. That's just a shell lying there.

They will pay. Every single person involved. I'm not a princess anymore. They'll learn I'm the fucking queen, and every single one of them will bow down to me and cower in fear before I destroy them.

And anyone who tries to stop what's about to happen will

regret the day they crossed paths with me, including the man holding me in his arms right now because every single one of them is to blame.

CHAPTER 1

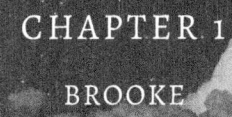

BROOKE

A FEW WEEKS EARLIER

*I*t's the first day of summer, and I'm here for it. I step out into the hot air, and the warmth immediately hits my skin. I close my eyes and take a deep breath. I can't wait for what this season will bring.

It's as though I can smell the ocean already. I can taste the salt spray from the waves on my tongue. I can feel the ocean water cooling my toes and hear the water lapping on the sand. Freedom—that's what it feels like, and I honestly want it more than anything.

I can't wait to leave Asheville. Don't get me wrong, it's a pretty town, full of old architectural buildings, there's a lot of history here. It's one of those towns where they would talk about the founding fathers in class at middle school. A bunch of old rich white dudes decided to build on this land blah blah, insert eye roll here.

The problem is, it's not very big, and there's not much to do. The highlight of a weekend is just another house party with people you've known for years or milkshakes at Benny's. Those are about the only two options for a "great" weekend. I grew up here, and as much as I used to love it, as I get older, I realize it can be stifling at times. I feel like I've outgrown it.

Does that make me sound awful?

It's small, not like a huge city, and everyone knows each other's business. It's frustrating as hell hearing all the rumors that were more than likely true, yet no one's business except those involved. Secrets here are hard to keep. That's the worst thing. You can never make a mistake without it being splashed all over the town.

I remember being at school and everyone's phones going off within seconds of each other as the gossip spread about whatever poor unfortunate soul stepped out of line that day.

And even though I'm not at school anymore, I still hear it. I even know that Jennie, the assistant at the local mayor's office, had slept with her dad's boss last weekend. I had never spoken to her, not once, yet I know everything about her private life. It's a little ridiculous. If Jennie wants to have a torrid affair with an older guy, good for her.

Hell, isn't that what I want?

I'm not about gossip. I never have been. I had seen how it ruined people's lives before; therefore, I guard my secrets well. The biggest one of all is kept hidden away. Not even Nate, my best friend, who knows all my secrets, knows that one.

Okay, well, maybe that was for a different reason besides not wanting to become the joke of Asheville. That secret haunted my dreams nightly. If it came out, everyone in town would know, and chances are it would destroy my best friend and others involved. I would never want that for myself or my friends, which is why I can't wait to graduate from college and leave this place.

I plan to move to a big city, one where I can get lost in a crowd and have adventures I can only dream of. I don't know which city yet. I figure I would close my eyes and point to somewhere on a map. The nearest city would be my new home.

I decided to study Drama and English Lit at college. I want to write when I get older and create worlds people can fall in love with, and I know I can write anywhere I want. My trust fund that kicks in when I turn twenty-one will allow me to live my dream without struggle.

We moved here from Chicago when I was five. My parents had lived in big cities their whole life. They had met in college, and it was love at first sight. My mother followed my dad from city to city as he built his media empire. They were now the third-largest media and advertising company in the US. When the business began to run itself, they decided they had enough of city life and semi-retired, though my dad still had a hand in making major decisions in the business. Ironically, they couldn't wait to move to a small town, and I couldn't wait to move out of one.

But this summer is different. Away from this town, away from the gossip, away from the dullness of my college life, away from everything and anything I could never want. Well, except for one thing. But that was one thing I could never have, and that was coming with me, anyway.

Nate, my best friend, had worked on my parents for weeks to allow me to go on vacation with him and a few others, and they finally caved on one condition. I could go if I wasn't the only girl.

My mother seemed to think me going on vacation with a group of boys meant wild orgies and drugs. I could only wish, but nothing that exciting or thrilling ever happens to me. Not that I would turn down an orgy with Chase, Asher, and Jax, even if I am a virgin. That would be way too hard to turn down.

So, I invited Harper, my girl bestie, and basically my sister. She had joined mine and Nate's dynamic duo a few years ago, and honestly, I can't imagine my life without her. She is utterly crazy about Asher, one of the guys coming with us, so it was an easy sell. They're not really talking right now though, their dynamic has shifted, I just don't know the reason why. I need to speak to Chase about it.

Her parents are away for business or traveling the world for ninety percent of the year, so no one is around to tell her no. Her family doesn't care enough to look after her, let alone tell her she can't go. I hate my overprotective parents sometimes, but I was always aware I would rather have them, than parents that didn't care at all.

Harper became part of our trio when we were juniors in high school and now attends the same college as us. She had come from another small town and instantly set her social status. Since small towns like to gossip, she announced everything she needed and wanted to say to everyone she met. Hard to gossip when everyone already knows everything about you.

I'll never forget how she just sat at our lunch table in the cafeteria. "You two look like the only people I've met today with a brain of their own. Friends?" The memory brings a smile to my lips. Harper doesn't give a crap about anything, and I envy that about her. She lives every day as if it's her last. To hell with the consequences. She's bold, loud, and knows what she wants, or maybe I should say who she wants, but that's another story.

Harper is simply stunning. Her long blonde hair always looks perfect, like she's spent hours on it, but I know differently.

It naturally looks incredible even when she gets out of bed. Half the time, she doesn't even brush it. *Bitch!*

She's just a little taller than me, but with how she dresses, you would think she's six foot with legs for days. I don't know how she does it, it doesn't matter what I wear; I always look five foot two. She could be a model but instead wants to be a designer. Harper's like me and wants to get out of this small town and follow her dream. She has the same bright blue eyes as Nate, and I sometimes wonder if she's his secret twin. There's a startling resemblance.

I exhale deeply, letting go of the tension and worries. I can't wait to just have fun and let go. The fact it was only hours away thrills me to the core.

A low chuckle breaks me from my fantasy, and I open my eyes, looking over to see my best friend. His golden blond hair shines in the sunlight, the easy messiness of it blowing in the breeze, and those gorgeous eyes that sparkle with teasing like usual. I narrow my eyes at him playfully. "What are you laughing at?"

Nate walks over to me, grinning—those dimples melting my heart—and raises his fingers to my cheek, pulling a loose strand of my hair out of my face and tucking it behind my ear softly.

"You're away with the fairies again, beautiful," he whispers, staring at me intensely, keeping his hand on my hair. Those bright blue eyes search deep into my soul, but for what, I'll never know. I smile, inhaling him as he keeps me close; he smells like sunshine and fall. I know it sounds stupid, but you know when you're outside as the summer winds down, but it's still beautiful weather, and the first leaves begin to fall? Well, that's when you know fall is here, and you can smell it in the air, and well, that's what he smells like.

Anyone looking in on this action would see a couple having

an intimate moment together, but not us. This is just how Nate is with me. He and his brother are weirdly tactile. I laugh, pushing him back.

"I was imagining the ocean, dick. I can't wait."

I playfully punch his shoulder, and he acts wounded. Holding his arm and pouting at me. That only gives him two reactions from me—a classic eye roll and a grin.

He chuckles again, wrapping his arms around my waist and lifting me up against his rock-hard body, spinning me around a few times. I laugh again, feeling free. I throw my arms out, enjoying it. He always gives me that feeling. I know I can be myself around him.

While he is six foot, I am only five-two, and when he picks me up, I feel like I am experiencing the world from a different viewpoint. One a lot more carefree and fun. As he drops me to my feet, I rest my hands lightly against his chest. His chest moves heavily, and the palms of my hands are rising and falling with each of his breaths. God, I swear every time I see him, he seems more muscular, with more abs, hard lines, and broader shoulders.

When I was younger, I willed myself to like him. His deep, bright blue eyes are like pools of water you can lose yourself in. His muscled and defined figure causes most girls to drop to their knees in worship. Football has made him built and ripped. Muscles ripple down his arms as he moves, and he's amazing because of it.

He could have had a football scholarship anywhere for college, but for some reason, he chose to go to the same college as me. It's just an hour's drive to the nearest city—if you could call it that—which is madness to me. I didn't even want to go there, but when it came time for college, my dad got sick with cancer, and I needed to be close to home. I sometimes wonder if he stayed because of me. He always says he has everything he wants here whenever he is asked.

Weird.

His soft, floppy, barely styled hair always looks perfect despite using very little product. Most days, he doesn't even bother. I hate that about him. He can just run his hand through it, and it is perfect. I love running my fingers through it. I can get to my knuckle before it disappears out of my hands. But the truth is no matter how gorgeous he is, how sweet and funny, I can't do it. I only have eyes for one man, and holy hell, what a man he is.

Chase freaking Anderson. Nate's off-limits older brother.

Six foot three, a wall of muscle, and a mystery to any girl he meets. He is hot. As. Sin. He is twenty-six years old, making him seven years older than me. Usually dressed in tight jeans and just a simple tee paired with a leather jacket. He always looks like he stepped out of a bad boy's GQ photoshoot. His eyes are bright green and almost crystal-like. They remind me of sea glass. They are haunting and draw you in.

Where Nate has taken after his mom, Chase has taken after his dad with dark brown hair that looks almost black at night. It's shaved a little at the sides, but the top is just a mess of hair. I've imagined gripping that hair multiple times and not in an I'm just your brother's friend kinda way.

His body looks like it was carved from a god's marble, and even though I love him in winter because he looks hot on his motorbike with his jacket and dark hair, I love him in the summer more.

I know he is out of my league, but watching him every year at the pool at Nate's house fuels fantasies that will last for years to come. Water dripping off his cut abs, his hair soaking wet, and that cheeky grin is utter perfection.

Last year he got a tattoo on his ribs, and holy fuck, I wanted to run my fingers across it, but I can never get close enough to figure out exactly what it is. But, needless to say, seeing a guy like him tatted only makes him sexier. That level of hotness should be illegal.

Rule one of the best friend code is you don't fuck your best friend's brother... At least, I'm sure there's a rule somewhere like that, and I had just said yes to spending six weeks in a beach house with him, his best friends, Nate, and Harper.

It was going to be a long summer, but the truth was, I missed him. He hadn't been around much lately, always traveling for some unknown reason, and I missed sitting under the stars with him like we used to. Growing up, he was always sweet to me, but lately, he has distanced himself from me, and I don't know why. Another thing I have to find out about this summer. I was starting to feel a little like Nancy Drew.

"Hey, Tink... Leave the fairies alone, yeah, and come join me here." Nate's voice breaks me from my fantasy of running my tongue up Chase's abs under the night sky, and I find my eyes meeting his. He's tapping my temple and giving me a strange look.

"I'm sorry, I'm just excited!" He wraps his arm around my shoulder and pulls me close. Picking up my suitcase, he leads me to his sleek black truck before loading it into his trunk. He loves this truck more than anything. It was a present from Chase for his eighteenth birthday, and it's his pride and joy. I've never seen him love anything more than his truck. It's an F-150 Raptor. Dark black with a custom glaze on it that almost makes it look holographic. It's a beast, and I love the roar of the engine whenever I'm in it.

Harper, Nate, and I often drive up to the mountains on weekends. My father bought a cabin up there for us to escape to.

We could have rented, but my father is crazy and sees it as an investment. Personally, I think he just likes to treat us.

As I put my hand on the truck door, Nate spins me around to face him, taking my hands and raising them between us near his heart. His dimples show again as he smiles. Those dimples are why many girls fall for him, and I can see why, even if I can't make myself feel it.

"This will be the best summer ever, Brooke. I can feel it. This summer is going to change things forever for us." I feel my breath catch as he stares at me with such intensity in his eyes, like he has a purpose, a mission, a secret I'm about to find out. He looks like he wants to say more, but he drops my hands instead and presses his lips to my forehead softly. "Now get your ass in the truck, beautiful, before I leave you here."

I laugh softly, wondering what he meant about this summer changing things for us and what else he was going to say before getting in the truck. I connect my phone to the stereo, browsing through my playlists before finally settling on one. I look out the window as the engine roars to life, and a shiver of excitement runs through me as we drive to Harper's house to pick her up.

Little did I know he was right when he said this summer would change things for us. He was so fucking right, and I never could have prepared myself for the things ahead. I wasn't ready and don't think I ever could be.